Yellow
Jeep

Eileen Egenolf

For my grandchildren,
who gave me the inspiration to write this book.
I love you, forever!

Yellow jeep, yellow jeep,
are you hiding in the fog?

We see you now, by
the black and white dog!

Yellow jeep, yellow jeep,
where are you today?

We see you now, beside the bales of hay!

Yellow jeep, yellow jeep, are you wearing a hat?

We can see now, it's a big, black cat!

Yellow jeep, yellow jeep,
it's 12 O'clock!

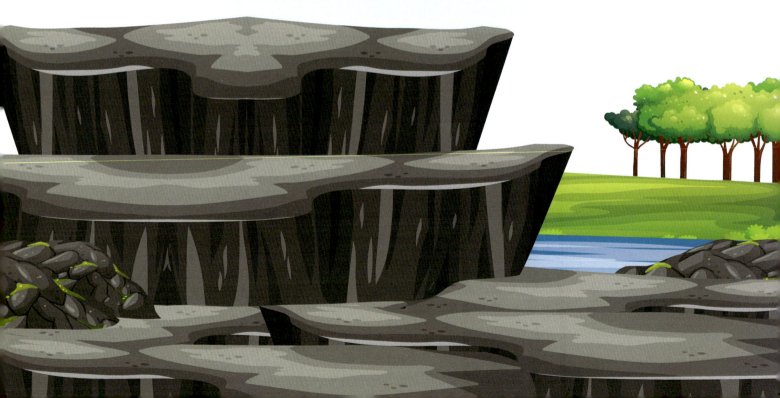

We see you now
up on the giant rock!

Yellow jeep, yellow jeep, where can you be?

We see you now behind the old apple tree!

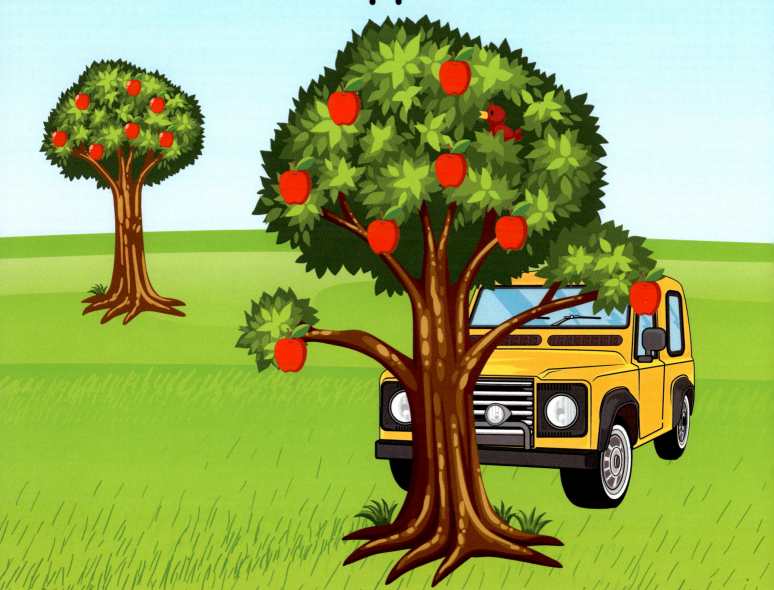

Yellow jeep, yellow jeep,
where are you at this hour?

We see you now in front of that big sunflower!

Yellow jeep, yellow jeep,
we hear a thud!

Yellow jeep, yellow jeep,
where are you now?

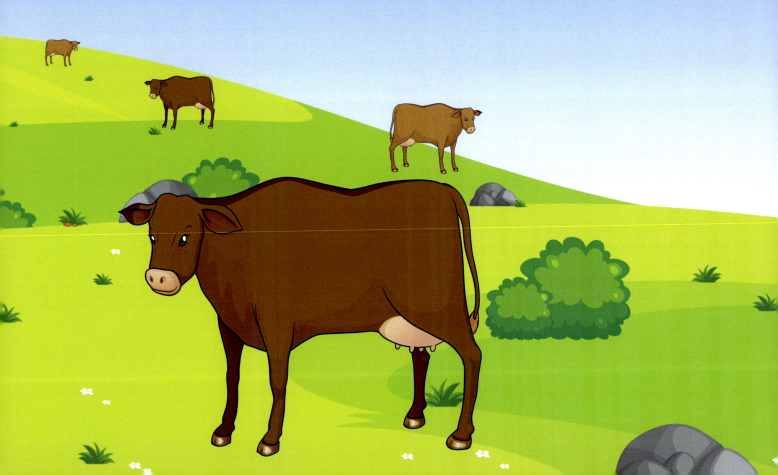

We see you now
behind the huge brown cow!

Yellow jeep, yellow jeep,
it's time to go to bed!